Gorwelion:
Shared Horizons

Robert Minhinnick is co-founder of Friends of the Earth Cymru and Sustainable Wales/Cymru Gynaliadwy. He published *Green Agenda: Essays on the Environment of Wales* (Seren) in 1994. He lives in Porthcawl.

Gorwelion:
Shared Horizons

Edited by

Robert Minhinnick

PARTHIAN

Parthian, Cardigan SA43 1ED www.parthianbooks.com
First published in 2021
© the contributors 2021
ISBN 978-1-913640-55-2
Editor: Robert Minhinnick
Cover image by Peter Morgan
Cover design by Syncopated Pandemonium
Typeset by Elaine Sharples
Printed and bound by 4edge Limited, UK
Published with the financial support of the Welsh Books Council
British Library Cataloguing in Publication Data
A cataloguing record for this book is available from the British Library.

This volume is dedicated to Alwyn Jones and Steven Harris,
who understood the value of education,
and combining science with the arts.

CONTENTS

INTRODUCTION

Gorwelion: Shared Horizons stems from an idea of Margaret Minhinnick's during summer 2020, acknowledging the declaration of a 'climate emergency' by the Welsh Government in 2019.

Today, even a culturally conservative council such as Bridgend in Wales has a 'climate change response manager'. My own '*gorwelion*' (horizons) are located within this county borough.

I began working in the environmental movement in 1980. I now realise climate change and the Covid-19 pandemic mean that politics for the rest of my life will be characterised by desperate, totally inadequate crisis management.

Nothing we are doing is appropriate for the urgency of this climate crisis.

Our volume's purpose is to acknowledge the importance of COP 26, the major conference on climate, taking place in Glasgow in late 2021. Thus we are delighted to include two leading Scottish writers as part of this project. Our Indian writers are invited for the global perspective they bring, together with acknowledging our charity's continuing links with the essential Fair Trade movement.

In 1994 I wrote: *... looking at what is occurring in Latin America, India, and the Far East, it can be confidently claimed that "the environmental holocaust" long proclaimed by science fiction writers and once-discredited doom-tellers, has already begun...* (*Green Agenda: Essays on the Environment of Wales*, Seren, 1994). Less than thirty years later someone would have to be a fool or deliberately obtuse not to acknowledge that holocaust is happening everywhere.

It ranges from tidal rising to the extraordinary loss of once familiar species, especially insects. It is manifested in droughts and wildfires, 'weird weather' and its consequences, population movements, 'climate refugees' and everywhere profound cultural change. Predicted for decades.

In June 2021, Channel 4 News reported that the UK government's own advisory body on climate change used 'its harshest language yet', accusing ministers of being 'shockingly unprepared' for the climate crisis.

The Climate Change Committee states that urgent action is needed immediately to deal with home insulation; extreme weather events, food supply and potential power cuts.

Greenpeace East Asia Forests and Oceans Project Manager, Pan Wenjing wrote

1

in 2020: *Global health crises like the COVID-19 pandemic will happen more often if we fail to protect natural ecosystems globally.*

As to the locations here, they include one of the most remote areas of Scotland and rarely-celebrated places in Wales. All writers were invited to focus on their immediate home areas, and consider the near future, together with that place's history.

Special thanks to Sampurna Chattarji for selecting and editing the contributions of our Indian writers. I find all of the Indian contributions powerful and everything I hoped for from this project: real, based on both past and future, truthful about what we are doing to the planet, with a fantastic mixture of cultural references and language (maybe only possible from Indian writers), surreal, science-fictional, terrifying, humorous (note Priya Sarukkai Chabria) and ultimately grievous beyond elegy. And achieved during the worst of the Covid-19 pandemic.

My original intention was to include *Gorwelion* in the Welsh language. Unfortunately, because of our deadlines, this has proved impossible. Sustainable Wales promises our second volume of *Gorwelion: Shared Horizons* will rectify this.

Robert Minhinnick, 2021

TISHANI DOSHI

Keeling Towards Water

I know the house I'm living in will one day be swallowed by the ocean. I cannot know whether it will happen in my lifetime, but there is freedom in this restlessness, that one day it will be gone. I fix my eyes to the horizon as though it could steady me. It is an instruction not to lower your roots too deep. The boundaries you've created are already broken in parts. Goats saunter in to graze through holes in the brick compound wall. The house fills with creatures. You lay out traps. You try to mend the walls. The ruptures come again.

I live on a spit of land on the southeast coast of Tamil Nadu in South India, halfway between the cities of Chennai and Pondicherry. The Bay of Bengal, a moody, majestic sea, lies two hundred feet from where the garden begins. Behind the house is another water body, the Buckingham Canal, where women stoop over to collect clams, and kingfishers and golden orioles flare like darts of colour. Behind this is the Odiyur lake, and stretching into the countryside in every direction, are a glittering network of lagoons, creeks and wetlands, which attract thousands of migratory birds. During the peak summer months of April and May, the land is scorched. Only the valiant put out their flowers: frangipani, flame of the forest, laburnum. The rest of the vegetation is brown-tipped, fatigued from the corrosive sea air. By the time the north-east monsoon hits us at the end of the year, everything is transformed, and life buzzes with this greening.

Visitors often comment on the air. How humid it is. How there's always a slick sheen between you and comfort. But the element that truly defines this place is water – the lack of it, the too-muchness of it. Flood, drought, tsunami, cyclone, failed monsoons, 'day zero'. We've had it all.

Before the British set up the East India Company in Madras (now Chennai) in 1639, the area that we'd call Tamil country was a network of agrarian villages, towns and kingdoms, connected by aquifers, irrigation systems, canals, rivers, marshlands, and a long sandy coast. From Rameswaram, the south-eastern-most outpost of this coast, the god Hanuman with his monkey army is supposed to have built a bridge across the Indian Ocean to Sri Lanka. Even the most water-deprived inland villages had wells and temple tanks; some over 1500 years old have been unearthed along with funeral urns filled with husks of millet and rice. Water has always been ambrosial here, connected to the land like a lover, the stuff of poems.

Since the 1980s though, water bodies have been clogged, drained, paved over to make way for high-speed roads and high-rise buildings, petrochemical refineries and power plants. One of Chennai's largest wetlands, the Pallikaranai marshes, which used to be a haven for several species of grass, fish and birds, has become a giant garbage dump. Before and after aerial shots of the marsh show it shrinking from 13,500 acres to 1,500 acres. From above, it used to look like an emerald bull flicking its tail. Over the years the bull has been invaded by plastic and landgrabbers, making it look like a lobe of cancered lung.

There have always been tussles between land and sea in Tamil Nadu. Forty-five kilometres north of where I live, the Pallava dynasty, which flourished from the 4th century, made their capital in Mamallapuram. They were master temple builders, many of which still stand, but six of the seven earliest free-standing temples that once dotted the shore were taken by the sea. Go further back to the famous Tamil Sangams, the legendary gatherings between poets and gods that supposedly lasted for thousands of years each, and gave birth to an entire literature. Two of the three Sangams are believed to have been destroyed by a great flood. Along every coast of this peninsula there are stories and myths of legendary cities swallowed by water, barters between sages and the sea god Varuna to relinquish land from the sea.

It's tempting to say that this is the cycle of things. Land must give way to water. But what we're living through is an unprecedented lurch into *piralayam,* the deluge and destruction of a world. All attention to geographical categorisations that used to exist, poetic or practical, have vanished.

The Sangam poets organised the Tamil land into five *thinnais* or categories (mountains, forests, pasturelands, seashore, wasteland), each with its own codified world of animals, birds, trees, prevailing emotion, soil, time of day, god. If they used the words stork or mango, pool or morning, you would know we were in *marutam*, the pastoral countryside, where lovers must contend with unfaithfulness and the predominant mood is sulk. If they spoke of nightfall, you would know we are in *neytal*, the coast, where there is unbearable waiting and anxiety in separation.

Studies about the agricultural practices during the Sangam period reveal that kings were deforesting large tracts of land and replacing sandalwood to make way for short-stalked rice, that there was a hierarchy of caste – the elite being landowners, with the majority divided into labouring classes. Land too was subjected to hierarchy depending on its ability to yield. But there were also spaces that remained outside the purview of the revenue register – groves, the margins around water bodies, grazing areas, pockets of land for village fairs and assemblies, burial grounds and burning ghats. According to Chennai-based environmental activist Nityanand Jayaraman, these free lands were *poromboke* areas, not a free-for-all like the European idea of the commons, but designated for certain communities at certain times. During colonial rule and after, these spaces were considered useless because of their uncultivability, so much so that the word *poromboke* became derogatory, applied to a person or place to mean worthless.

And so those 'worthless' margins around precious lands have now been appropriated by Information Technology corridors and desalination plants. Over the past two decades, Tamil Nadu has lost 41% of its beaches to erosion triggered by coastal infrastructure projects. The land's ability to withstand floods has decreased, not just because of the unrelenting construction, but because contractors are building over existing drainage systems that have existed here for centuries.

Growing up in Madras, I used to have a recurring nightmare of a giant tidal wave sweeping us into the clouds. Over the years I moved closer and closer to the sea. Now that I can hear the Bay of Bengal breathing at my gate, that dream strangely has not returned. I put water out in clay pots for the birds, and after watering the fruit trees, my dogs nestle in the cool patches of wet under the branches, making me feel as though I should be doing the same – finding a safe place to shelter.

I read about the curlew sandpiper, a tiny thing with a wingspan of a little more than a foot that has flown 6,000 kilometres from the Siberian tundra for its yearly frolic in the mudflats of Vedaranyam further down the coast. I think of the clay idols of the gods we immerse in rivers and seas after festivals, sending them on their journey home. The idea of return is a potent one, but some years the estuaries turn dry and the mud flats will not form. The clay idols have mostly been replaced with plaster of Paris, so, for a long time now, the gods have been poisoning our rivers and seas. Birds and gods can travel between homes, but coastal communities can't. What happens when one home is lost? What happens when you only have one home?

When I think of the future, I cannot think of just the square mile of land around me. I have learned from the Sangam poets that even though I am a person of the sea, I cannot be disconnected from the person who lives in the mountains.

5

Categories are always porous. A jungle hen may one day find itself in the desert; a lover could slip through the cordon of paddy fields and find his way to you. Those poets showed me how the landscape we inhabit becomes the grammar by which we decode our lives – emotional and ecological zones that might allow a person to navigate her inner feelings with the world she sees reflected outside. How by doing this she may find her feet, her heart, which is always keeling towards water.

MAGGIE HAGGITH

Assynt

I live alongside about a billion barnacles on the shore of Loch Roe in the northwest highlands of Scotland. Poet Norman MacCaig declared it 'this most beautiful corner of the land'. The two long sides of our 11 hectares are the edges of a peninsula, Roinn an Oba, which means 'ploughshare of the bay'. It points southwest into the prevailing wind, carving the waves into furrows as they roll in from the Minch, the stretch of sea that links us with the outer Hebrides. On a good day here, Lewis, Harris and the Shiant Islands stand clear to the west, Skye lurks away to the south and to the north there's nothing but sea between us and the Arctic.

Down on the Roinn, up to three dozen common or harbour seals and a couple of Atlantic greys slob out on whichever side is most sheltered from the wind, spreading themselves in gangs between the shore and the bos and skerries scattered across the loch, which are upholstered by bladderwrack and embroidered on their peaks with scurvy grass and thrift, among which geese, oyster catchers, eider ducks and terns squabble for nest sites and attempt to raise chicks despite the appetites of black-backed gulls, ravens and otters.

I come often to swim here and never a day goes by when I don't have companions in the water – as well as the barnacles waving their feathery legs, there are cormorants, dabchicks, black-throated divers or mergansers and always a heron, flapping off with a disdainful prehistoric squawk, making me feel I owe her an apology for disturbing her and thanks for the grace of her presence – after all it has been a heron home for far longer than it has been mine.

The rock cracks are packed with shell fragments, broken bits of mussels, limpets and periwinkles, the detritus of countless meals of gulls, otters and herons, built up over decades or even centuries. For the rock itself such timescales, indeed anything realistically imaginable in relation to human experience, is so fleeting as to be irrelevant. The rock here is among the oldest in the world: this is Lewisian gneiss, three billion years ancient, grey mostly, but sometimes thrift pink or charcoal black, depending on its minerals, and hard, obviously, having resisted erosion by all the forces the planet has thrown at it since long before it came up with the idea of life.

These rocks have seen all the climate changes earth has yet devised, experienced every conceivable severe weather event, lain under sandstone mountains built several kilometres thick by sedimentation, capped by quartz and limestone, all scraped away by ice, eroded off by frost and snow, washed clean by rain, laid bare again now after three million millennia as a geological foundation for this magnificent landscape. The gneiss is here to stay, whatever happens to the climate.

A moth alights. Over time it has learned perfect camouflage. Under the waterline, barnacle spats cement their foreheads to the gneiss's certainty and settle in for the rest of their lives. After twenty-two years I know I too am here to stay, trying to blend in, not do too much harm.

Ever since I first moved here I've been making an effort to live lightly – off-grid, compost toilets, veggie patch, you get the picture. This is a corner of the world where life and capitalism slow down a bit. Nonetheless, it's still the first world and the nearest petrol pumps are going strong: there's not much sign of us reaching zero carbon lifestyles anytime soon.

Given that we're still contributing to human-induced climate change, what's the impact likely to be here? The difficult to stomach truth is, not so bad. The salt marsh at the shore may become inundated when sea level rises and depending on how fast and how far it does, the beach, the fabulously-flowery machair grassland and the car park behind it could all end up underwater. There are a couple of houses pretty close to the shore, but most are built on higher ground, of which there's plenty.

Yet there are signs of change in the ecosystems already – fish movements are different now than in the past, for example. People talk about shifts in the weather – the jet stream seems to track further south sometimes, bringing us more Arctic air, though the big radiator of the Atlantic Ocean still tends to thaw us out fast.

As for increased storminess, this environment is already well adapted – the trees are raked by sea breezes and gales and no one builds a door into the west wall of a building. Some of the diverse life here may face change, have to move or adapt, but it has been doing that for countless millennia. The next generations of barnacles and humans will just have to cement themselves a little higher up the rocks. There is great resilience in the diversity we have here.

The likely future reality is that we'll be a bit wetter – will anyone notice? – and a bit warmer on average, and that, to be honest, will make this place more, rather than less, clement. We might be able to grow grapes or walnuts, not just brambles and hazels. This is the cruel and sickening injustice of climate change. We are not like farmers in the Sundarbans, whose low-lying fields are at risk of being inundated by salt water, rendering them infertile for years afterwards, forcing already poor people into destitution. We are not like south sea islanders made landless by rising seas, nor drought-stricken sub-Saharan Africans, nor Arctic peoples whose ice habitats are melting out of recognition.

We, unlike polar bears and the bulk of poor people on the planet, are not really at risk from climate change. What changes arise here are not likely to be at all life threatening. We, this wealthy country, have caused a global problem we will not suffer from. Compared to most people on earth, for us here, the living is easy. I wonder if the future will bring us climate refugees and if so, I hope we will be as welcoming as we should be.

For a while, this square mile, which is already mostly water, will become a bit more watery. And then, at some point in the next few thousand years it will probably freeze back over. Ice will scrape and scour the land clean of all the mess we humans have made. The gneiss, unperturbed, will be the foundation for whatever may come after. Long after human beings have done messing with the place, it will still be glittering in the last rays of our dying sun, still glowing in the fading moonlight, hosting without judgement whatever beings muster themselves, offering solidity to all of life's various and beautiful softness. And I bet the barnacles, fluttering their fluffy little legs, will still be right here too.

ROBERT MINHINNICK

Ffynnon Wen

Name: Ffynnon-wen Rocks, Bridgend (Pen-y-bont)
Place type: Other Coastal Landform
Location: Grid Ref: SS 7985 7877 • X/Y co-ords: 279858, 178770 •
Lat/Long: 51.49509811,-3.73205478
County/Unitary Authority: Bridgend (Pen-y-bont)
Country: Wales

1.

A life,
of sorts,
undoubtedly a life.
I live it at the waves' edge
in the white quartz...

That life spent listening to shells...
But how else should I spend my time?

Salt around the pools today
like chalk where the dead bodies lay.
Yet somehow
a promise will be kept.

Towers of smoke above this beach,
its clints and grykes all rains might reach.
But wait....
                    Were there volcanoes on the Gower?

2.

I've been to Pompeii and seen the last bus arrive,
its timetable scorched under an inch of ash,
the slaves
    buried alive,
the prostitutes
    buried alive,
the gladiators
    buried alive,
the dogwalkers carrying plastic bags
    buried alive,
the sunbathers smeared in factor 40
    buried alive,
the lifeguards with their highlights and Samoan tattoos
    buried alive,
the brawling boys and their silver whippets
    buried alive,
the philosophers in their caves
    buried alive,
the girl who sells Mivvis and Magnums and Soleros
    buried alive.

And not all of them two metres apart.
Thank the gods
I always wear a mask.

3.

But who are the people
who build these driftwood shacks
and lie with the bonewhite dead
we all must become?
Are our children
the fossils of the future?

Might be
millennia ago
or a part of next year's
fairground pixels.

Yet a life, of sorts,
undoubtedly a life
lived at the waves' edge
in the white quartz...

A hut for one night...
built from driftwood and the sea's plastic.
Yes, something once flourished here.
And might so again?

The cults will rise and rule and fall away.
Eons it might take
but eventually
each tribe returns to its territory.

Sandstone like blood under the sea
and veins of quartz that have led me here,
but who are these people
building with sticks white as ivory?

4.

A life
of sorts,
undoubtedly a life,
lived at the waves' edge
in the white quartz...

Now and then and now and then
golf balls and jellyfish at Ffynnon Wen
towers of smoke above the steelworks beach
or the scalding rain
   and burning light
of the Vesuvian night...

Salt around the pools today
like chalk where once the bodies lay

and no way back
until this driftwood reassembles itself
– its sticks white as ivory =
and we can all lay ourselves down
amongst its terrible
bones...

LAURA WAINWRIGHT

Airbrushed Fields: Newport's Glebelands

HC

grows roses
round her door.
River roses
burgeoning

in audacious sprays,
shouted shapes.
HC. Insignia
of an intersection imagist.

Stealthy as the evening Usk,
between motorway lights,
caught in the drift,[1]
the uprising mud,

her half-empty canisters
rattling like the HGVs
crossing concrete
bridges overhead.

HC, I'm sorry.
This mural is mine;
your school-book hearts
and pink stars

paint you in my head
when it is day,
the sun is warm
and I know nothing

in this place is as it seems.
These lush, airbrushed fields
are palimpsests too

their stories
metres deep.

'O to blot out this garden/ to forget'.[2] Standing again at the same 'door' – an echoing gap between austere concrete motorway-bridge columns in Newport's Glebelands Park – I was struck by how familiar and transformed my surroundings appeared. Two weeks without rain and the river was much lower, lethargic; the previously muddy bank, with its almost metallic patina, now baked hard and fissuring; the window of sky over the streaming carriageways above me a more disarming blue.

And HC – the initials and the mural – had vanished; overwritten by ballooned Bronx-style ciphers. I would have questioned whether they ever existed, were it not for the photograph I took on my phone at the time (like many people, I now seem to need digital proof that I have set foot anywhere), and one rogue pink star – a junked satellite, caught in orbit. As the essayist Brian Dillon writes:

> *erasure is never merely a matter of making things disappear: there is always some detritus strewn about in the aftermath, some bruising to the surface from which word or image has been removed, some reminder of the violence done to make the world look new again.*[3]

Graffiti and street art is palimpsestic and iconoclastic by nature, of course. And perhaps this was all the work of a single artist, with multiple personas. But I felt personally invested in HC's story, as I originally perceived or imagined it; suddenly philosophical in the face of such creative obliteration.

The area of parkland, playing fields and motorway underpasses in east Newport known as 'The Glebelands' is founded on erasure. In January 2009, a local newspaper ran a story with the headline: 'Newport recreation ground closed after toxic find'.[4] Council investigators had confirmed that corroded barrels and evidence of PCBs [polychlorinated biphenyls] had been found in an area of the park, close to the river: a 'bruising' to Glebelands' benign 'surface'; a quiet 'violence done to make the world look new'.

Glebelands is, in fact, an old rubbish dump – what Newport Council call a 'civic amenity', or what is identified elsewhere as 'an uncontrolled landfill', site. Consequently, as the Council website states, the ground in this part of the city is 'prone to sinking slightly'. And when I walk there I am indeed aware of an unusual give in the earth (whether real or imagined); an almost spongy sensation underfoot.

Information about exactly what or how much waste is buried at Glebelands is scant. Indeed, no official records appear to survive at all. According to one source, however, the materials interred below Glebelands' green facade include 'everything from household waste to animal carcasses and a wide range of hazardous industrial chemicals'[5.] such as the PCBs discovered in 2009.

The latter were used historically in paints, dyes, adhesives and plastics; transformers and capacitors; electrical devices, hydraulic fluid, flame retardants, and thermal insulation materials such as fibreglass and foam. They were banned in the 1970s in Europe and the USA when scientists linked exposure to PCBs to a range of health conditions in humans and animals, including cancer, diseases of the immune, endocrine and nervous systems, and congenital disorders.

PCBs are also harmful to the wider environment and its ecosystems precisely because they refuse to disappear. They do not decompose organically. Instead, they endure, seeping from industrial and landfill sites into the environment and the food chain.

To the north of Glebelands Park there are allotments where local residents grow vegetables and fruit. Glebelands is also the controversial location of a new primary-school building, which faced considerable opposition from environmental groups and concerned parents before its construction was finally approved. Arsenic, mercury and ammonium were among the pollutants found in the soil where the school now stands.[6.]

It is difficult to believe that toxins from the entombed material at Glebelands have not found their way into the muddy currents of the Usk – a river supporting a plethora of wildlife – and on downstream to the Severn Estuary; 'the many-foamed ways/ of the sea'.[7] Levels of PCBs, in particular, are known to be especially high in river sediment, on flood plains and on the seabed. Indeed, these chemicals have been detected in some of the most remote and uninhabited locations on the planet.

One scientific study revealed that levels of PCBs detected in amphipods in the Mariana Trench – the deepest oceanic trench on Earth – were equivalent to those found in Suruga Bay in Japan, 'one of the most polluted industrial zones of the northwest Pacific'.[8] Researchers believe that these accumulations of PCBs are the result of contaminated debris, particularly plastics, and dead marine organisms, sinking to the ocean floor. If, as climate scientists predict, the planet warms considerably this century, sea levels continue to rise, and serious flooding becomes commonplace, just how far and at what depths will the invisible 'detritus' of Newport's, and other cities', industrial histories be 'strewn'?

I stepped out from the chilly shadow under the motorway and into the sunlight. Glebelands' fields and scrubland were top-dressed with atomised April colour. A mistle thrush sifted for worms amongst the daisies; and bees rummaged in the dandelions' deep yellow pile. In the hazy distance, four crows congregated like match officials on a halfway line. A child ran over the soft grass in bare feet.

When I went back to the park a few weeks later I saw that HC had also retuned. There it was, that solvent signature: two cobalt-blue letters scrawled further along the wall. I felt both strangely reassured and jolted. I have not gone away, they seemed to say. I was just sleeping.

[1] H.D., 'Sea Rose', in *H.D. Selected Poems,* ed. Louis L. Martz (Manchester: Carcanet, 1997), l. 8 (p. 3).

[2] H.D., 'Sheltered Garden', in *H.D. Selected Poems,* ll. 54-55 (p. 5).

[3] Brian Dillon, 'The Revelation of Erasure', in *Objects in this Mirror: Essays* (Berlin: Sternberg Press, 2014), pp. 309-316 (p. 309).

[4] *South Wales Argus,* 30th January 2009.

https://www.southwalesargus.co.uk/news/4087661.newport-recreation-ground-c [accessed April 2021].

5. Glebelands Alliance. http://www.chepstowfoe.org.uk/glebelands/abt_glblnds.htm [accessed April 2021].

6. BBC News. http://news.bbc.co.uk/1/hi/wales/south_east/3237224.stm [accessed April 2021].

7. H.D., 'Hermes of the Ways', in *H.D. Selected Poems,* l. 10 (p. 14).

8. BBC News. http://www.bbc.co.uk/news/science-environment-38957549 [accessed April 2021].

PETER FINCH

The Holy Power of Penylan

Fy milltir sgwâr, my personal square mile just outside my door, is not as large as a mile in any direction. Nor, come to think of it, is it anything like square. None of them are, these special places, these backs of hands, these tracts of local land that you know so well they patina your skin and flow through your veins. Mine is mostly hillside, steep in parts, one that I've known all my long life. I was born here. Just pre-NHS. In a private nursing home run by a Mrs Jones. My parents, as economically challenged as most in this black-and-white period immediately after the War, rented places to live. Rooms. Offered out among the terraces spread across northern Roath and southern Penylan.

Around 1950, they moved up in the world and joined my mother's family, the Davises, and settled for what turned out to be most of my younger childhood, in the rambling communal house on Tŷ Draw Place. Aunts, uncles, cousins, rollicking piano in the front room, chickens out back.

Now, after decades, I've returned to the same stamping ground, to live in a place just up the hill from the Tŷ Draw house at Bronwydd. This newer house is built on land that was wood and field when I first knew it. Paths through the trees with a spring emerging from under a tumble of masonry near the top.

On the tithe maps from the early nineteenth century, the land is shown as almost empty. The fields of William Jones' farm. My house is built in the centre of one called Waun Fawr. Just to the south are fields bearing the names Pump Erw y Castell, Waun Firion Grobos, Dwy Erw, Cae Canol, Cae Crwn, Cae Ffynnon, and Cae Firen Per. The Welsh mangled softly but at least there. The contemporary replacements are The Willows, Silver Birches, White Lodge, Garth, Woodland Rise and Tŷ Gwyn House: *White House House*, such a splendid resonance in its bilingual echo, they named it twice.

On these early maps, up where Eastern Avenue rolls through along its deep cutting, was Penylan Well. A Holy Well. A spring of ancient power with a history that goes back, folklore tells us, to the birth of Christ and before. The shape of our Lord's knee is pressed into the well's rim. There were Easter fayres held here, around the well, to celebrate its unearthly powers. Oxen were spit roasted. Drink drunk and dances had. The raves of their day. You could get the well and its holy water to act for you if you made the appropriate offering. A pin bent and thrown in, your sacrifice, a strip of your clothing torn and tied to a nearby bush. If it were disease you wished cured, then the illness would seep from your body in time with the colour bleaching out from the cloth strip under the south Wales sun.

These pagan pre-Christian wells were commonplace right across the land. Some still stand but most are forgotten, the powers they had ignored. When Christianity arrived, rather than face down the older religions, it merely took them over. Work for Christ not against him. Around Penylan Well, hymns were sung. Delve into the folklore and you'll find tales of veneration but also stories of ghosts. Men on horses. Women in dark dresses wailing and moaning in the darkness, trapped here by love lost, by ancient wrongs, by things which can never be put right.

When I went hunting for this bubbling source of holy power, I laid maps across each other, ancient and modern, and found the precise location: the north-western corner of the Jewish old people's home at the burgeoning Penylan House. The trail of exuded water from the spring had been let into the drains, allowed to seep through the earth. I followed the course of its gully south, running through the back gardens of the Bronwydd houses before disappearing in the direction of the Nant y Lleici, Roath Brook, running alongside Roath Recreation ground.

I told a neighbour that at the back of his garden seeped holy water. Things grew powerfully there. He told me that he'd put it to good use. I've no idea if he has.

During the corona incarceration, I've spent time walking these streets. These empty Ballardian places. The sense of otherness leaking through them, the feeling that the world has ended here and time has become frozen. Ballard's youths stand in the shadows, holding their skateboards before them like Roman shields. The world is tilting slowly, the light passing across it with no-one to notice. Does it cross if it is not observed? Does this madness only persist when I see it, does it only stay when I write it down? Above the ridge there is smoke. You can't see the fire. To the north, the valley heads have all been set alight by the disaffected and are burning south in scorching churn, leaving a deep red smoulder in their wake.

Did I leave any marks?
Having time, I start a hunt for myself, for anything that I can connect to. These were my places, after all. I'm as old as anyone else. Are my footprints still held somewhere like those of the dinosaurs along the Barry coast? I'd walked down the lane at the back of the house at Tŷ Draw Place, looking for the green paint I'd

spilled or maybe my name penknife-carved somewhere, and found nothing. Shapes are familiar, the lane follows the geographic line it always did but there is nothing of me there. Not anymore. I've raised that ghost memory and run it through my head so many times that by now, in 2020, it no longer sparks. Even I am beginning to forget what it once meant. The Romans had a quarry nearby, did they not? Full of fossils and water, a horse, a chariot and hoards of golden swords slung into its mud. There was a railway too. Smoke and smuts. Industry. Coal. The twin cooling towers of the power station at Colchester Avenue to the south. The world turning. Now it just sits.

The meadowland that my house is built on was once part of a farm managed from a house called Tŷ Gwyn. Collectively, this was Tŷ Gwyn Penlan Farm, on land owned by the Marquis of Bute. The farmhouse, the white house that much of the district celebrates, is long gone. The third Marquis, John Crichton-Stuart, who had converted to Catholicism in Southwark in 1868 and wanted to leave his charitable mark on the world, gave a slice of his land to the Congregation of Our Lady of Charity of the Good Shepherd. In 1870, they replaced the farmhouse with a convent, a house of mercy for fallen women. 'Penitents and girls in danger free. Ages accepted 13-50. Places 130.' The new mothers worked in the laundry washing the clothes from the district's great houses. Magdalena Laundries, for that it was this was, were not happy places. In 1871 the third Marquis had his architect Burges design and build a chapel where a barn had once stood.

The whole edifice of distress and God-aided despair came down in the 1960s to be replaced by Heathfield House School. Today it is clean and pure and massively well attended as St David's Catholic Sixth Form College. The multiracial pupils arrive by car and coach, whoop up Tŷ Gwyn each morning, all phones on speaker. Life still here, Magdalena gone.

The district's great houses are gone too. Early on in the industrial revolution, they dotted the hillscape. Great places that were the properties of shipping magnates. Their roofs would have wrought-iron viewing platforms from which the Docks could be observed. Ships arriving could be spotted. The state of the tides discerned. Penylan House, Oldwell, Hillside, Green Lawn, Shandon, Linden, Graigisa, Fretherne and Glenside are all no more. Demolished and with smaller properties often developed on their land.

Bronwydd House stood where Eastern Avenue cuts through. It was owned by Sir Alfred Thomas, Mayor of Cardiff, and before demolition, donated to the city and used as a children's home. The one great house that remains is actually not all that great, and neither is it that old, which, I guess, is why it remains. This is Cornborough, built for the shipping magnate, arts lover and philanthropist, William Reardon Smith. Reardon-Smith owned a shipping line. One of its ships was called Cornborough. Which came first, ship or house? I need to find out[1].

Across the world, history might be in retreat, hiding from the statue defacing mobs and those bent on changing its names. Doesn't matter much if that happens here. There are no statues, no plaques. The names have all been managed by the passing of time, in any event. They have been changed at a whim, altered to fit prevailing circumstance. But, despite assault, history remains. The curve of the drives, large enough for a hansom cab to turn, the slight depressions in the ground where the streams once flowed. A metal bridge side that marks the passage of a railway. The haze in the air, the sense of place, this place, that hovers still.

Where do we go next?

Where do we go next? Into a future irradiated with contemporary belief? The Dan Dare future of floating space platforms, 1950s rocket ships and free and frequent trading interchange with the Therons from Venus and the fast-walking stick people from Mercury. The rising sea future where the planet submerges. Eryri is the last of Wales before the water sinks it. Of the world, all that remains, is the plateau of Tibet where belief in the moment and the breath of the Buddha might save us yet. The Ballard future of overbuild, of endless, seamless conurbation that runs on into the next street and the one after until it eventually finds its tail and eats itself coming back. That one has the mountains removed to give us more space and the oceans drained for farmland. The whole Gaia made artificial and screaming. The Cardiff Booster future where we win the tourism war, build an airport off our coast, and attract more trade than the rest of Wales put together. We become the centre as if we are not that already, and we hold. We throb with money and power, which naturally begets more money and power. Caernarfon moulders. Môn sinks slowly into the Irish sea.

Actually, none of those.

We are a small place, after all, and we need to celebrate that. Big is not necessarily better. Small is actually beautiful. It matters not at all that just over the border, England, with its megaphone directives, has spent the last two-hundred-and-fifty years blasting us into silence. Envy does not become us. We need simply to not listen.

In Wales, we should be better placed than most to weather the post-Covid future. Our virus figures out there in the green desert have been historically low. We've been the adopted home of Leopold Kohr, whose pupil EF Schumacher wrote the ground breaking *Small is Beautiful: A Study of Economics as if People Mattered* in the early 1970s. Small is an inherent Welsh quality. The idea of doing less and doing it more slowly is deep seated here.

The open democracy campaigner Anthony Barnett has outlined the next steps which, up here *yn fy milltir sgwâr* and the wider Wales which surrounds it, would suit us well.

Fix health as a right for all and not as a system constantly responsive to market forces.

Allow all nations to be equal and insist they are democratic.

Oppose the rampage of neoliberalism and authoritarian capitalism. Their time could well be done.

End 'the dismantling of veracity' and return to that place where the told truth was paramount and you didn't alter things just in case they might upset someone.

And, perhaps most importantly, replace globalisation with humanisation. Cease our frantic destruction of species and our off-the-scale encouragement of climate breakdown. Our overbuilding. Our manifest proliferation. Be people again.

Saying these things to myself as I walk up the hill, just to check them out before I write them down, it all begins to sound a little unobtainably utopian. Aren't these aims little more than a future fictioneer's fantasy? Ridiculously unavailable. I wave across at my socially distanced neighbours, out taking their government sanctioned exercise, much as I am, but on the far side of the road. Maybe. But when I examine them, all the alternatives have flaws and, in order to stay alive, I have to believe in something.

[1.] Out of the Belly of Hell: COVID-19 and the humanisation of globalisation. Anthony Barnett. https://www.opendemocracy.net/en/opendemocracyuk/out-belly-hell-shutdown-and-humanisation-globalisation/

PETER FINCH

Heading up Ty Gwyn with Allen Ginsberg

A solid mass of Heaven, mist-infused
Same breath as breathes thru Capel-y-ffin
Wales Visitation 67
Same year I saw him checking Better Books window on Charing Cross.
Meets Dafydd Rowlands at Laugharne in 1995. He tells me that.
A bard in a land of bards.
Up here the guarded face of the United Synagogue top of this street.
Mezuzah on the doorframe.
Opened one of mine on Bronwydd. Unrolled the prayer. Felt the magic infusing
the palm
Ginsberg complaining about his legs pulling up the Ty Gwyn Vortex
Old men on the holy hill
But not afraid

SAMPURNA CHATTARJI

Last She Looked

[19.2233° N, 72.9630° E]

[INCREASED STORM INTENSITY]

When the wet came, it was feral.

Thick-tongued and circling it fell upon the paving stones where the cars lay, still as bleached bone.

It was the cyclone passing on from Kerala mutating into this soup that fell out of the sky.

It wasn't yet time for the wet. How did dust turn into rain, wet into sound, giant into dwarf? Wasn't this the dry time – the scandalous time when slopes caught fire without a human hand?

Those fires were once manually lit – `biodiversity damaged by man-made forest fire, April 5, 2019` – bursts of flame that sent primordial shudders through her heart as she watched from her dark balcony – big enough for one folding chair and an entire expanse of sky.

She had been sitting there for years, growing old as the hills.

At first there was nothing. Nothing human that is. Not even swamp. This was not bogland like her other city grown out of marsh – bodies planted in the marsh to grow noxious and sprout their tales into the ears of children, the mouths of garrulous cabbies. That was Kolkata. This was – not even Bombay, but Thana – Thane.

Thane that reminded her of Macbeth. Thana that reminded her of prison.

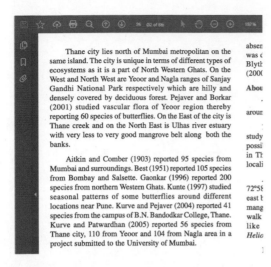

Her tiny uncaged balcony eyrie-enough on the 6th floor. That was how clear the path had been before her eyes.

First: the tremendous rain-tree whose pink flowers stood erect each evening.

Second: the scrap of ground, communal, with both its meanings, where MHADA kids played wild games, and small farmers spread their moveable feasts each Saturday.

Third: the forest. That was what it was. Not yawling with bikers. Just forest, silent and unnameable as the hill that looked like a giant lying on her side.

[BUNDLES OF STRESS]

Then came: the smokers, the chewers, the male urinators around the *paan*-shop nailed into the bole of the rain-tree. The snack-shop blistering the smell of Kolkata Rolls, out of time and place, into her nose. Wrapped around the tree, two-tiered Speedy Asian, woks that spoke into the night, way past civilisation.

Then came: the cricket pitch poured onto the ground, and watered, as if it were a garden. Concrete slab where pigeons fed on scattered seed each morning, secret parking spot for a solitary bike and, at sundown, battlefield for sparring cricketers.

Then came: the felling of trees, the hewing of road, the sudden springing of passageway, the privilege of cars over leopards, now caught only on insomniac cameras, signalled by the petrified howls of pi-dogs, white spotted ghosts looking for food in their own backyard.

For she lived in their backyard, didn't she? She was their tenant. And they asked no price except some privacy to hunt and feed at will.

With the sinew torn out of her haunch, she flickered like haze, her crippled giant.

Yeoor. What did this ancient word mean? She searched and did not find. What she found was mythical. Changeable Lizards. Indian Migrants. Angled Sunbeams. Granite Ghosts. Ditch Jewels. The Chocolate Albatross. The cloak-

and-dagger bee. Tickle's flowerpeckers. Robberflies. Lunar Moths. Albino Crabs. Were these her neighbours all along? Why did she never see them except on screen? What was a hood with not one neighbour to be seen?

The air inside the stertorously breathing denizens as curdled as the one that hung outside their iron-grilled windows, their barred doors.

Nobody moved.

[SUBSTANTIAL INERTIA]

Yesterday, the second dust storm whipped through the place that once bore branches (she can see them still, X-rayed into her eyes). Orange light billowing like oedema.

Chained to her bed, tubed to her concentrator, the gurgling sound of bubbles a kind of warning.

What lies to the right of her balcony where she never sits anymore because the coils don't reach that far?

Last she looked it was leaden.

Around the vast warehouses, abandoned for twenty years, machines had worked their way through the green, torn the monkeys out of their trees. They arrived on her balcony, bewildered and yammering. There were snakes everywhere. She had looked through the gap-toothed wall and seen the woman who had bought the whole land, a corporator's wife, plotting high-rises.

They never happened. The disease stumped them.

A triumphant laugh emerges from her throat.

Along the motorable road – so proudly displayed by ignorant new inhabitants as a mark of distinction on this 'godforsaken place that was not even Mumbai' – all she heard was sirens. Artery that bled to the hospital. Only two places left anymore. Home and Hospital. By 11 a.m. everyone who was still mobile would crawl back in. You would hear the voice of the megaphone scolding errants on the lurk. For those who had no one, the municipality sent helicopters. There. Copter o'clock, the time of the food packets, *poi-bhaji*, and one pouch of chlorinated water. She has hired an urchin to collect hers and leave it outside her door, stained and warped by gone monsoons.

She can see the neem trees, their bitter leaves plundered to cleanse all ills, save one.

She can see small white and pink florets, twining their way along the once-new road, punctured by broken bottles of alcohol.

She can see gardeners, hired by the municipality, the life-giving chores of their

27

small brown fingers, their careful watering of flowerbeds, into which hired dog-walkers planted their thick-soled boots.

She can see women plucking public flowers for their private shrines, open acts of thievery.

She can see – around the bend where morning invariably took her – the misbegotten sculptures – giant ladybirds, livid sunflowers, one misshapen tortoise. Monstrous consolations. Inside the park named after Namdeo Dhasal, poet of Kamathipura, Gol Pitha, poet of brothel and rage, she can see yogic islands, contortionists, laughers, prayers, oblivious to the two masked ladies sweeping the paths of fallen leaves and yellow blossoms, their daily act of grace.

She cannot see further than that.

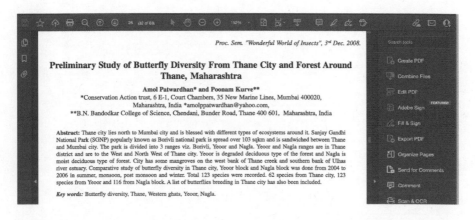

She had once walked all the way up to the village on top of the hills, past the Air Force Station. If she kept walking, she would have reached the other end of the reserve. The Sanjay Gandhi National Park where scrawny lions were displayed to people in caged buses.

She remembers the drop in temperature the instant she entered the gates from this side of Yeoor 60 square kilometres of deciduous degraded by anthropogenic activities Buffer-zone prickle of cool on skin, trees named by meticulous foresters Fifty-feet trees! High undergrowth! Signs that said what the birds 2365 species, 13 new ones sighted on 21 Jan, 2015 and the butterflies 123 species! looked like Rounded Pierrot Vindhyan Bob Absent in Thane City Common In Yeoor! where the wildlife lived 157 species, as per the last nisarganubhav machaan census conducted by the Maharashtra

28

Forest Department on Buddha Poornima: night of the full moon, May 20, 2019, 13 machans of people standing on treetops and counting the numbers, commoners and experts alike – why oh why had she not been one of them?

She remembers the huge rocks, the winding path clinging to the landmass that later she would regard only from her perch. There was the spot where a Major had been killed by a leopard. He had risen too early and walked into the forbidden before the sun was up. He had trespassed and paid the price.

She, they, all the hunkered down denizens, had trespassed too. No price they paid could be enough.

[IRREVERSIBLE BREAKDOWN]

She whispered as she fingered the green bedspread that was all that remained, reminded of habitat. Here, the circles of harvesters. Here the women with the sheaves, the women stirring cookpots, cradling babies, here the peacock strutting, here the pots of water astonishingly balanced on heads, here finger millet, cane, barrow, crop. And here in the centre, the blower of the *bhopu*, cornucopia to his lips, last remainder of bounty, reminder of once-was, where now nothing-is but drought and parched lip, a blighted land, 44.4 kilometres north of the Arabian Sea which eats away at the city once known as Bombay.

She shifts her fingers to the braille of her *kantha* top. A gift from her marshland mum. Green as the cover she lies on. On it the entire landscape of her other land. She sees bent horses, vigilant owls, wag-tailed dogs, travelling fish, the archer, the drummer, the pounder of pestle-and-mortar, the growing *lota-pata*, the world as it once was.

There is no life long enough.

When they find her body, they will lift her off one memory and place her onto another.

The flame will burn clean and bright.

The urchins with the black garbage bags will rescue the remains.

Someone without superstition will wear lush Bengal on her torso, *dhono dhanye pushpe bhora.*

Another will wrap herself in the whirling Warli dancers of Maharashtra, great state, down on its knees, her giantess broken, Beetle Colony, Ant Pagoda, Three Seasons, names of human constructions built out of sand.

ABEER AMEER

Sapling, 2031

'If the Day of Judgement comes
and one of you has a sapling in your hand
you should plant it.'
– Prophet Muhammed

It's been years since she paid such attention
but this sapling consumes her thoughts, is her sanctuary.
The whole world in a pot. For now, her fears are forgotten.
She turns to this olive tree to be. Just like when
she was eight years old, sitting by the pond
in their back garden of the bungalow in Heath Park Avenue,
looking for air bubbles or movement beneath the lilies.
A different shade of green in her favourite body of water.
She'd catch a newt, notice its smooth skin and delicate feet,
place it carefully on the rock beside her.
And, in Baghdad at the age of eleven, she'd search for geckos
along the roasted walls of the flat roof in Karrada.
A different taxonomy, yet so similar. *From the same family, almost.*
Absorbed by the flame-shaped buds and leaves of this little tree,
she knows that it's just another part of the same family.

The air seems as close as the first time
she deeply heard birdsong.
Her great uncle Muhammed's garden
in Al-Qadisiyah, Baghdad.

Late August,
an hour or so before dusk.
The sun yellows walls, lengthens shadows.

A garden hose on the ground,
running water trickles onto cracked earth,
between strands of beige-green grass.

The birds, so many birds, drink water
in see-saw tilts. Swifts and sparrows
thank the Maker of water, the owners of the hose.

She sits with her father in the garden,
his first time back in Iraq after twenty-five years.
The return after the loss of his parents. And so much else.

Sitting there in the garden with small glasses
of sweet cardamom tea, date and pistachio pastries,
they speak of many things.

Her father retells the stories she knows well;
of outrunning rabid dogs in the cemetery, of shaving
his head bald to stay home for shame of failing exams.

How he fell for pranks played by her mother
each April Fool's Day: the sixth pregnancy,
calls from Immigration, a few fake robberies.

Amu Muhammed chuckles. It's a sound she savours;
a reminder of her grandfather.
One of the few memories she has.

Her father becomes quiet, the creases
in his skin smooth over.
A distance in his eyes.

He turns with his whole being and smiles:
Listen!   Listen!
How beautiful!

She was a child when she sat on the rock
beside the garden pond in Heath, imagining newts
warning their offspring of humans. All the while
Chernobyl spilled its radioactivity.

A child when images came from Halabja
of other children gassed to lifeless plastic.
How the world must have always seemed

so hopeless to adults. Her parents, grandparents,
uncles and aunts; how they must have worried.
She never noticed. They hid it well.

Yet, since 1991 she has measured each year by loss.
That year she became a crow,
her clothing black, her face ashen.
From her throat
            a croak
to carry the weight
of many strangers' making.

That year, all her trees were weeping willow.
Shadow was the fragrance she wore.
Her dark eyes glazed in guilt.
        Heavy metal
was the weight of her heart,
its discord crashing upon her
like the replay of the news clip:

US bombers strike civilians in Amiriyah shelter

She thought she saw her grandmother
among mourners for the dead. 408 dead.
The screams from the bunker stopped
                except in her mind
and struck a gulf between her and her friends.

A calligrapher of elegy,
she forbade all music from her charred ears.
A blackout of light and joyful sound
only to let in the mourning night
to this thirteen-year-old's crow heart.

It's twenty-thirty-one.
If the Day of Judgement comes
and one of you has a sapling in your hand
you should plant it.
She comes back to this saying often.
Since she was thirteen, The Future has been
the scariest thing, the darkest place.
Her amygdala conjures and avoids in equal measure.

She returns to where she grew up, what is left
of the streets she had walked with her mother.
Past where the red postbox used to be, Highfield Road,
    down the slope,
across the weak bridge where they picked blackberries.
Not quite the mulberries of Baghdad,
but they always transported them to the Tigris banks
before they continued to Roath Park Lake.

Those buried behind the black gates and Star of David
of the Jewish Cemetery
    have witnessed many
        more scarred strangers here.

None of them are that far from Srebrenica.
It seems closer with each headline.

Now the streets she walks
are more like the weak bridge they used to cross.

It seems to her that life has been a repeating cycle
of separation   of worlds ending
                              and beginning
                                        again   and   again.

As they used to say in Iraq
Makaanhum khaali: *Their space is empty*
she notices what's missing:
the twittering wheeze of greenfinches
their yellow and green,

and the song thrush.
Hedgerows barren, deep in melancholy,
      without that mixtape call.

She wonders at her parents.
Her father's ability to hear birdsong
when birds have gone quiet, when he sees nothing.
Her mother, lighthearted and effervescent,
though distance has broken her heart many times.

He still tells her to *listen*. She still tells her to *find joy*.

It's not just about the lost music.

What human hands do,
                    the seas and earths tell.
Winds and storms already rage
in obscured skies
                    soon too steep   for birds to fly.
      The air already too thick
                    for them to sing
                    as the sun draws ever closer.

                    She digs a hole into the ground
                takes the olive tree sapling in her hand
                            and plants it.

34

ADITI ANGIRAS

That Thing with Feathers

Unearth. Opposite of earth. To dig and discover. From the depths of darkness, to bring to light. It is a phonetic cousin of the Sanskrit word *anartha*, which means 'without any meaning'. A calamity, a catastrophe, an action so grievously wrong that it renders everything else meaningless. Worthless. As if the opposite of earth was not discovery but senselessness. We've been seeking purpose in the stars and the skies ever since we got here.

Discover. From the Latin *discooperire*, to reverse the complete covering of something. When NASA scientists discovered buried lakes under the dry ice surface of Mars, it seemed unworldly. Unearthly, but with the potential of being earth. Like if we could just reach out and scratch the surface deep enough, we might touch something alive. The dead waters so saline that they would rub salt on our wounds if they could. The water left its birthmark on the planet's skin, a reminder that it once was, it once was a twin. Such light years are closer than they appear in the mirror, it would only take one birth cycle to reach *there* from *here*.

My city is halfway Mars, part-time paradise. Landlockedlandlockedland locked land. It's got nowhere to go. We've swallowed the key, along with a thousand lakes, a couple hills and a river. Now we've got nothing to do and nowhere to go. We switch on our windows and see the world pass by in black and white. Pigeons perched on the horizon, paused like ancient statues in a ruin. The sound of sirens fills the streets with a pulse every now and then. From the telescope, I look at the drop of blood in the sky and like an angry eye it stares back at me.

I grab the red pill and wash it down with a blue glass of water. They say that before colour began to disappear, Dilli was dream-like. A disco in the trees, birdsongs in the evening light. Two years after independence, the painted stork began to visit the *Purana Quila* and started a love affair with the lakes of the city. Come September, the canopy of the city would turn into a canvas of feathers. A winter's ball, with guests from around the world, from warblers to dancers, princely names and every spring shade under the sun. Just to call them by their names would make your throat blush with surprise. Coppersmith barbets, purple sunbirds, red-whiskered bulbul, bluethroat thrush, the greater flamingo, wood sandpiper...

Birds, busy globetrotters, their wings carry wireless letters from the future. Time travelling canaries in this coal mine of a city, now worm-eaten sonnets sing in their beaks. At the airport of today, their flight status reads: Delayed. Cancelled. Temporarily suspended. Harbingers of news that our feeble human brains don't yet know how to read. Our ears deaf to the dial tone, no vitali organ to warn us the vitals are dropping low. Soothsayers who can pick up frequencies mid-air, somersaulting seers whispering truths in the wind. They're leaving us, stranded on this island of buried lakes, obsolete. This subscription is no longer available in your location. Please try again tomorrow. The groundwater is asking us to dig deeper into our souls. Roots are crawling out of concrete pavements to walk us home.

They say that before colour began to disappear, Dilli was dream-like. A disco in the trees, birdsongs in the evening light. Now all I want from the future is the past. To unearth a thousand lakes, a couple hills, a river and a beating heart.

Dilli from the Urdu *Dil*, meaning 1. heart, 2. home, 3. spirit to brave the world.

This city carries the fortune of a dozen forts but has forgotten their wisdom. The hipster haunt of *Hauz Khas* translates into 'royal lake', wellspring of the citadel around Siri Fort that now lies splattered like a slimy rotten egg. *Dhaula Kuan* was named after an old well with white sandy water. Sand has turned into stone, and the splash has hit rock bottom. Now as you lean over nothingness, you can hear the penny drop. Abandoned like an ancient temple, the stepwell of *Agrasen Ki Baoli*, once a stairway to heaven, now sits idly, a hundred and eight steps to nowhere.

Can you imagine what a glorious sight it must have been back in the day? In the days before yesterday, when each pillar could see its own reflection in a pond? The map of Dilli is soaked with memories of water. The water never forgets and the land never remembers, this is the only tragedy. I can smell the stench of the *Najafgarh Nala* in my morning tea and afternoon nap. By evening, you get used to it like a pheromone. They plan to resurrect a bird sanctuary in this drain, but fear that the passerine flutters will interfere with the hum of pilot planes.

Buried. From the Germanic *bergan* which means 'to protect', the word stands tall like a fortress. Something kept aside, safe for later. Is the future being buried like a graveyard or a gold mine? I am light years away from it and understand that hope is different from optimism. After all, hope is the thing with feathers. Hope floats on water like a lullaby and dances to the hymns of the birds and the bees. There's always a glass half full where there is a glass half empty. Maybe hope is just a parable, a poem, a proverb. Now all I want from the past is a future. To unearth a thousand lakes, a couple hills, a river and a beating heart. Dilli from the Urdu *Dil*, meaning 1. heart, 2. home, 3. spirit to brave the world.

SUZANNE IUPPA

To Aberangell

The tawny owl starts calling just as it gets too dark to make out shapes through the window frames. It sounds so close, coming from the woods, right into the back garden.

It's not been raining today and it will have good hunting with the wood mice, coming to eat the blackberries in the hedges, as I have today, and I have been able to collect the cooking apples where they have fallen with today's strong breeze. The hollyhock which was blooming so beautifully in its pot on the terrace has fallen off, fallen several feet in the garden below, and snapped. I found it when I went to gather windfall apples for my supper, and bring the dry laundry in from the line on the ridge underneath the Clipiau. The mountain's name, under which my cottage nestles, means 'steep hillsides'.

Recently, Storm Francis passed our valley over. We had no power for just over nine hours in an area with no main gas supply. The villages of Corris, Mallwyd, Aberangell and Dinas Mawddwy had dark skies indeed. Several trees down, as you would expect; seeing some of the several hundred year old oaks felled, root-plates exposed, the all-important veins and arteries ripped through, as if the trees need to be re-wired.

That is sad, and feels like a defeat. It is soon forgotten as no one has been hurt and there are several people who will come with trailers and chainsaws and partake of free hardwood for their winter fires

My roofer rings me to catch up and arrange to come take some details for repairing my dormer bedroom window. Living on the ridge at the back of the village, my roofs are still being rebuilt from the storms last February, which flooded many of the valleys in Wales. I did think of the trouble we caused here with so much run-off at the head of the huge Welsh rivers. I can see Pumlumon from my back terrace, the mountain which is the watershed source for the Severn, the Wye, and the Rheidol.

I moved to the upper Dyfi at the time valley four years ago. I lived in Flintshire in a border market town for twenty-five years prior, raising my three boys and working as an environmentalist. After my children grew up, left for university and started their own families, it did not feel right to stay in the family home. I needed to shed a skin.

At the time I was working for the Vincent Wildlife Trust, supporting grants and partnership work for the historic 'pine marten recovery' project, to establish a breeding population of our native mammal in 'southern Britain', using translocation as a conservation tool. After a tracking expedition for these animals in the surrounding Cambrian mountains, I translocated too, finding a small quarryman's cottage and terraced garden, south-facing and looking down the valley.

I am also a writer, of short stories and poetry, with an interest in pilgrimage. My stories concern the Age of the Saints in Wales, and different materials which were mined from the earth – slate, lead, coal. Thus, if you were to overlay with translucent maps: one of the most secret, wild parts of present Wales, another hosting our short spate of heavy slate mining, and another holding an important 'braich' (branch) of the Cistercian Way, you would probably find my village, Aberangell.

This is a confluence of two rivers, the Dyfi, which is the country boundary between Gwynedd and Powys, and the Angell, which does mean 'arm', or perhaps 'talon.' Friends from Carmarthen, incredible civilisation by my standards, say – Oh, you live in that place no one's ever heard of. I beg to differ; there are whole families here with the surname Angell. Television naturalist, Iolo Williams says – Oh yes, Aberangell is where I go to look for goshawks!

Yes I do have a roosting goshawk in my garden and now, a local pine marten makes an appearance every so often, taking out the occasional grey squirrel in a loud extermination bid in the regenerating trees behind the hedgeline. I live on my own now, but I am surrounded by creatures.

It was quite a culture shock moving to this area, even though I had lived in Wales for 26 years previously. I didn't understand the culture, because I didn't know enough of the language. I was interested in legends and stories, but didn't have a taste of the geography behind them, or the earth from all the different regions of Wales ground into the soles of my boots.

I had the knowledge of the fauna and flora, but I didn't understand how 'traditional' farming practices were impacting ecosystems in this part of Wales. If you are trying to learn about 'traditions', it's hard to be critical of them at that same time – or at least it is hard to enunciate those thoughts aloud to the community that is sharing their time and thoughts.

Their time and thoughts are precious. Although I am enjoying learning more about the language, geography, and farming practices, I've understood from living here that traditional does not mean ethical. Perhaps it never, ever has and that is part of the tradition. I think the hill farmers here are more concerned with

39

surviving; and Aberangell is not chocolate box farming. I've heard more than once from my neighbours. 'The views do not pay the bills.' Traditionalists will be challenged to come up with new land-use routines soon enough, post-Brexit. It's what they voted for.

This village has had a steady stream of 'incomers' since the late 1800s for the slate quarrying work, and then from the 1970s, with the development of nearby Centre for Alternative Technology, which is reached by taking a high pass (originally a monk's trod) over the mountains, from the village, through Aberllefenni, and down into Corris.

Thus for at least one hundred years there has been an odd mix, not really emulsifying, of Welsh hill farming, chapel, and the sung, spoken and written language (William Morgan's Welsh bible translated from Greek and Hebrew, was revised in 1620 at nearby Mallwyd by Dr John Davies); English midlanders incoming for work, and the eco-hippie crowd, seen as counter-culture, wanting a sense of place and community that focuses on living in harmony and consuming fewer resources while living a good quality life.

Good quality means: good family connections, a friendship network; community response to illness, hardship or threat, a local economy which can offer housing, food, means of travel and chances to make new partnerships. Connection with nature and growing and dying with the seasons is an overarching frame to it all. Do the traditional Welsh hill farmers or the eco-hippy counter culture have a better quality of life in their communities here? That is up for, often, hot debate.

There are still lurid red signs up along the Dyfi, further downstream as you leave Machynlleth, 'YES TO CONSERVATION – NO TO REWILDING'. The irony is you can't get much wilder than river ingress both summer and winter, and the year-on-year spreading phalanges of flood plain.

Our problems are likely larger than our newly introduced beaver population will be able to sort out, but I am glad they are working away out there, doing their own thing.

Local, innovative enterprise will surely grow, but as we have understood with recent rains we will have to devise ways of growing food in a wetter and windier climate. I think this is an exciting chance for the whole community to work together towards a common goal – food security.

Now that many people's commuting habits have altered in deepest rural Wales, it seems that radical change is possible. This will require reflection, not reaction...

I think we all feel significant change is coming, in our slatey bones. ....*Ymlaen*! (Onward!)

CHRISTOPHER MEREDITH

Steampunk jungle

I Steff, Cwmtawe 2017

That hot day
when the ridge in perpetual shade
even that ridge bulging above us
sweated and steamed
we walked you and I through
the hot mash in darkness
where they ripped up the railtrack
and the river was sunstruck
and brown through the trees
and the streams off the mountain
the paths and the ditches
were black with dead waters
and huge beeches and oak dug
their toes in the black scree
that urged them to slide and
to topple and crush us
we walked you and I in
the drowning forest
in the lattice of darkness
and splashes of sunlight
that lasered the canopy
and *look* you said *look the marsh orchids*
and mechanical as lampposts
they lit up the walkway
to that branchtangled shrine
in the steampunk jungle
a gibbet with pit boots
a pit lamp and battery
a hard hat on a post like
a skull in a story

dead flowers old snapshots
and felt pen endearments
this makeshift memorial
to those four last miners
maybe the very last
to drown in these mountains
in black mud and stone
and we passed fallen tunnels
like broken gods gaping
smashed chapels of engines
in ivy lianas
and amid the racked forest
a pylon surged upward
out of the bramble
the fern and the knotweed
and mineral grew scaly
and xylem and girder
and soared overhead in the
palæozoicoanthropocene
and *look* you said *look*
and there in the rust rills
that ran from the mountain
among roots and rail ends *look*
and there was the cracked cog
of some great machine
and with mud rusty fingers
we hauled it from water
the massy half disc of it
hand thick and fluted
precise notches locking
on sweating air
and we carried it down to
the still living river
and washed it where alder tongues
lapped at the water
we washed it this relic

this fragment of hubris
and didn't know then there
was no hand that made it
this fibre made iron
this fern from the hot swamps
from the ages when sweet air
bred marvels and giants
and oh my dead fathers
my burning earth's children
who forced me to witness
it never was crushed to
the carbon that killed us
and we didn't know then
it would wither in sunlight
and crumble to nothing
this tree before time
and over the drumrush
where river beat boulders
we heard the mad traffic
still roaring for murder
and a pterosaur heron
wheeled over the river
and a dipper too beaten
for flying or diving
fell down to a rock in
the seething brown waters
and spreading the cross
of herself on the stone
she grew still

PRIYA SARUKKAI CHABRIA

Report from Erandawane

LOCALITY: ERANDAWANE, PUNE, MAHARASHTRA, INDIA

Significance and History

Erandawane was named after a sacred grove of tall cork trees (*Millingtonia hortensis*) that spiked the night with fragrance sweeter than jasmine, shed by long-stemmed white flowers which hung in pendulous bunches as the monsoon receded.

About 120 years ago, mango (*Mangifera indica*) orchards replaced the grove. Sixty years later, squat homes appeared in the mango orchard.

Around forty years ago, bungalows gave way to a succession of four-storey buildings, and by-lanes.

A few remaining cork trees ring the mini park where, each morning, a few aged khaki-clad right-wingers gather to salute the Motherland. Covid-19 decimated the group.

Three small but well attended temples and numerous roadside shrines attest to my religious past.

Changes to Flora and Fauna 2021-2031:

1. Insects of all type have proliferated (Read my report 2010-2020) having found new breeding grounds as apartments fell empty due to fall in rentals in said pandemic. Further, the children of the dead, settled abroad, prefer outright sale but buyers are rare as economic recovery did not occur as per government predictions. Also, buyers prefer gated communities. I have by-lanes with independent buildings shaded by aged trees.

2. Pigeons (*Columbidae)* have declined. Several, though, were discovered roosting in the house of the late Dr. Ray and his sister, Ms. D Ray whose bodies were discovered three days after their demise in said pandemic. Thereafter, their building's unofficial name is Pretha Pigeon Palace or PPP; the postal address remains

Sri Ram Terraces. Ms. Ray's *pretha* is said to haunt the apartment, which residents of the building wished to exorcise. The local feminist group objected to this gendering of a possible ghost and the matter ended without a resolution.

3. Indian ringneck parakeets (*Psittacula krameri manillensis*) largely of the same generation as the previous decade – though greatly reduced in number – continue *to visit* surviving mango trees. Their favourite haunts remain the gardens of two priestly families, B. Purohit and V. Purohit who periodically conduct Vedic yagnas in their backyards which are livestreamed to clients abroad.

4. Three generations of Indian palm squirrel, (*Funambulus palmarum*) have passed. However, the next generation's high-pitched squeaks still awaken the neighbourhood. The kindly Mr. S of 'Belle Vue' who died young, undoubtedly helped preserve this species by feeding pups which fell out of dreys made between false ceilings and illegally extended sunroofs.

5. Cats (*Felis catus*) continue to thrive. Between February and August, the yowls of queens and caterwauling of tomcats prevent resident humans from getting a good night's rest. The ginger Kat gained a reputation for slinking into houses as neighbours, leaving doors ajar, visited each other to borrow groceries, while her tree-climbing daughter Kitty sprang from branches into kitchens when cooks were on their mobiles. Legendary is the genial Silky who did not stray from under her master's bed, the dearly beloved aforementioned Mr S, during his last days. 'Superfecund', Silky produces litters with regularity, thereby ensuring that all the cats here carry her genes.

6. Dogs (*Canis lupus familiaris*) except for a few pets, are strays. Popular among them was the late Cham–Cham–Chameli. Mr. Gokhle of Swastika – admired for its sacred tulsi (*Ocimum sanctum*) bushes – named her after a prostitute in a Bollywood film for 'being available to every male dog'. Cham–Cham–Chameli was sterilised, fed by

residents and protected by the Nepali security guard Mr K Vishwakarama of 'Belle Vue'. The recent rise in pet dog population is a contribution of the Tendulkar family's sudden prosperity. They redeveloped their orchard of coconut (*Cocos nucifera*), lime (*Citrus aurantiifolia*), guava (*Psidium guajava*) and banana (*Musa acuminate*) trees that surrounded their crumbling bungalow into Tasty Mess n Mall. The joint family reside in penthouses here with their dogs: two Huskies, one Pomeranian, three Alsatians and two Tibetan Terriers. Tasty Mess serves only one dish, missal pav-bread, in three variations: Hot, Hotter, Hottest, much appreciated by students of nearby collages. Each of the Tendulkars now own cars parked in the basement; male strays have adopted this car park as a dozing place between rounds of scavenging the Mess's garbage bins. Inspired by this success, other take-away joints, Soups-n-Sweets, Grannie's Goodies, Best of Best etc. opened, squeezed into the space of illegally felled trees. When the sparsely visited showroom, Glory Furnishings burnt down, it reopened as Punjabi Italian Cuisine. After the pandemic, the habit of ordering in food has continued unabated.

7.   Soil: In the last decade my soil condition deteriorated as every road, pavement and plot was concretized from end to end (though periodically dug up to lay cables and bumpily re-concretised). This was accomplished by the local politician to win votes. She succeeded, securing for herself a third term, enhanced security and two additional cars. However, it adversely affected my aeration, permeability and requirement to synthesize enriching rot. Organisms like earthworms (*Moniligastridae drawida),* snails (*Achatinoidea*), frogs (*Hoplobatrachus tigerinus*) and snakes (from *Naja-naja* to *Ahaetulla*) have all but disappeared. Daytime temperatures have risen; tree roots have weakened. My groundwater has reduced, forcing humans to procure water from tankers to meet their daily requirements. They resorted to keeping fewer house plants; now fewer bees *(Apis cerana indica)* and sun-birds (*Leptocoma zeylonica*) attend my locality. Nevertheless, humans continue to affect blindness about the consequences.

It pains me to end my decennial report on such a note. Therefore, I will strive to put things into perspective. The adage 'There is more to it than meets the eye' applies to me in significant ways. For instance, though I am perceived as still, I travel at incredible speed. Add to the earth's rotational speed that of our solar system spinning on the outer rim of a pinwheel galaxy which, in turn, is whirling away from other galaxies as the universe expands and it is clear that the next time I present my report I will, unknown to all, be billions of kilometres away from my current location.

NOTE: Names of participants of all species are changed to protect their privacy.

MIKE JENKINS

We Will Be Oaks

These people are insane: they represent the intense paranoia many of us are experiencing, but in a weirdly distorted form. They refuse to recognise reality, just like climate change deniers.

I wrote those words in my diary at the time of the great Covid crisis of 2020-21, about the anti-vaxxers, the so-called freedom movement.

I was totally right and also totally wrong.

Years on, what they said about the pandemic is reminiscent of those who denied global warming, yet ironically the totalitarian states set up then have been made so much easier to implement since, just as they envisaged.

As I gaze out on my wilting plot in the height of the Dry Season, I wonder how we let it happen.

I succeeded for a while in training that patch of clay soil to bring us fresh vegetables; with topsoil and also horse dung from nearby roads it yielded potatoes, cabbages, carrots and lettuces.

Now my garden's like the exposed base of a *cronfa ddŵr*, but a treasury of the dust and ashes of our nation.

It seems strange now, in our yearly floods and fires, how we pushed for our independence as water became our oil.

Coal, iron, copper, slate ... when they needed us they'd take it away leaving us with ruins and museums which chronicled our demise.

Then we began to emerge from our slumber: wind, solar, tidal and rivers all harnessed, though too many profits going elsewhere as ever.

But before we could vote, before we had time to say – 'We're old enough to stand up, be counted; mature enough to go our own way' ... it happened!

The new valleys flooded, the pipelines and long summers of drought.

It was all for the common good, like the wearing of masks and social distancing we'd come to accept in those plague days.

Could we sit back and let our fellow humans perish?

And before we knew it the armed forces were there at the crucial building sites and reservoirs, just as they'd been mobilised for testing and vaccines.

Harrowing television coverage of wasted crops and families being shipped bottled water. Our mountains and rivers were the modern oil fields of Iraq and Afghanistan, though the invasion was far more subtle.

We did challenge them.

They were turning Cwm Darran – once a pit valley and for so long a country park and lake – into a reservoir.

Our protests, our banners, our summoning of Treweryn – '*Nid yw CYMRU ar werth*'. There were thousands of us marching, chanting. Our red banners filled the roads to Parc Cwm Darran, coming to a halt at the entrance where machine-gunned soldiers defended the site.

Deri would be drowned. It was one small village, one small sacrifice they said. The media shamed us: they sing while others die of thirst.

Now even here on the mountain we worry as our water's piped elsewhere. There are stories of corruption we circulate as best we can given restrictions on social media: of tankfuls exported to rich Arab regimes whose rulers are friendly with royalty. It seems like the famine in Ireland: food exported even as the people starve.

They discredit us with tales of violence, of bombs in the night. (There may well be lone operators, but it's not the movement. Perhaps we are misguided and force is all they understand?)

We have our own water-tanks and irrigation, catching the rainfall in the Wet Season as people once scrabbled for pieces of coal on the waste-tips.

For a while it feeds our small patch, but when it's gone the sun's merciless.

The sun is like Sir Swanner, Prime Minister of New Britain, the man who saved the country (though not mine, submerged underwater). It tolerates no answers. It is relentless.

How did this happen when we had so much momentum, here in Merthyr and throughout Cymru itself?

We embraced new schemes of hydropower and electrification; even the eco-houses were beginning to be built... Till the climate turned against us, like an enemy who'd always been sniping, but now came out into the open brandishing weapons.

Spring and autumn shrank like tubers in the ground.

Whole species were driven mad by it: geese and ducks migrated in hot summers and never returned. Reservoirs were strangely devoid of wildlife, making us suspicious.

Infiltrated on social media, we turned against each other. Those who accused

49

us of selfishness did have a point. Those who insisted (as John Jenkins said, from his prison cell, of Plaid Cymru) that we were merely pacifists with no solutions, were equally correct.

They used Nature as they'd used people in their great empire; pitting one against another, exploiting our differences yet, ironically, appealing to a common humanity.

Is there any way back from this?

There was a time we lived in harmony with the bees who inhabited a nest at the side of our dormer roof and from our bed we could hear, all summer long, buzzing like the sound of a distant ocean.

With the many months of constant rain they went away. We have *hiraeth* for their sound.

In our garden, the oak still stands taller than ever, branches telling many weathers beyond our two-season year; its roots reaching down deeper than laid soil and packed clay; its bark, moss and acorns still sustaining many birds and squirrels.

We must be druid-oaks and reclaim the fleeting autumn and spring; burying our roots in this occupied land, despite everything.

NABANITA KANUNGO

A lost animal shares my history

It is March. Roaring winds sweep through the dry dusty lanes, broken by long awaited, too-brief showers. The horizon can be seen only from the terrace. I take a long look at Nongrah, the eastern flank of Lum Heh, literally, the High Hills, across the Umkhrah River, and try to listen. What I hear, above the river, is the nocturne of the pine's doleful susurrations, pierced only by the occasional howl of wolves on those nights of ghost stories that shaped my initial fear and thrill of the unknown.

I was five, or was I six? I remember how my mother would indulge my eagerness to do some 'heavy' chore, handing me a tiny toy kettle as I tagged along with a group of women going to collect drinking water from the river. I would sit at a safe height on a large stone and watch the women chatter as they washed clothes, took dips. Before returning home, we frolicked in the crystal-clear water, green with the reflection of mature pines and wild cherry trees along the slopes. Afterwards, we would relish a spicy salad of *Soh Phoh* or *Soh Shang*, their Khasi names as sweet as their taste, or wild pears from someone's orchard. On the way back, my pockets would be heavy with rounded stones collected from the riverbed – pumice for cracked heels. At those rare spots where the water assumed some depth, men could be seen angling, still and quiet as the stones on which they sat. The sharp, transparent clarity of that water still holds my memories of Diwali – my grandfather setting afloat a miniature boat made of plantain stalk, laden with little oil-lamps – an annual ritual for the peace of our ancestors.

Those hills, now shorn almost entirely of pines, are a tangle of concrete; the river, a large drain of sewage, foam and garbage.

> *I was born in this need to re-figure everything one has*
> *on geography's leathery skin, history's long tongue.*

In the fifteen years of my love affair with poetry, I have perhaps not been so preoccupied with anything more than romancing dead and passing landscapes. The sight of a clump of green has invariably touched me; brought me closer to centeredness. In a clumsy back-room of my mind, my words rehearse their dumb performance for that one shining moment of communication – the neighbourhood I was born and grew up in; a place which is also time, an answer as much as a question – as to why one might turn to a tree, a river or even the plants in one's garden with the desperation, guilt and longing of a lover; why one mourns and commits to an unrelenting search for a lost arboreal world of berries, hedges and nameless flowers; why one could be afflicted with the passing of a taste; grieve the sight of a stunted peach or plum.

What strips my search of its seemingly nostalgic landscape-gazing is the mantle of history my neighbourhood broodingly bears. A past that lurks around the corner to ambush me – one of the third generation of refugees from erstwhile East-Pakistan – with curt questions. For instance, being asked to leave my job as a teacher in an institution that was my alma mater, solely due to my ethnicity.

Our house in Shillong – one of two-hundred-and-seventy-five others, allotted by the then Assam government to Bengali Hindu refugees from East-Pakistan – was built in 1953 by my grandfather with his meagre earnings as a clerk in the North-East Frontier Agency. After many legal disputes, the name of our 'colony' was eventually changed to 'Relief and Rehabilitation Colony' though informally, there are many who still refer to it as 'Refugee Colony' – a denotation in which it appears as though time were frozen into a singular frame of ongoing violence, and continued disruptive change. It is tragic how it never seemed strange that we had grown up being identified as a *dkhar* or 'outsider', absorbing insidious, less obvious honours of a perpetually operative othering, through the anxiety of months-dragging-on-to-year-long curfews imposed as a fallout of ethnic riots. The neighbourhood would go eerily quiet on those nights, pitch dark, sleepless, apprehensive of the next episode of stone pelting, rape, lynching, arson. On such nights '...*the language of welts rising slowly on the panes, / a cracked blur of riot-torn air...*' left one wondering which year it was. Was it 1947, 1979 or 1992? And where in this country's map could one locate a place that seemed to want to disappear out of shame?

I vividly remember listening to traumatised screams from across the river as the sheds and tenements of cattle and owners alike were hatefully razed to the ground. I remember the day when a group of armed local youth came in a van and nonchalantly painted the words 'Refugee Colony' in bold, black tar-laden strokes on the wall of the community hall. I remember how it did not surprise me that no one came out of their houses to see what the noise was about. The boys left shouting slogans: Foreigners Go Back – a slur that, inflicted to this day, has become banal despite its associated indignities. Auden's scathing poem 'Partition' (1966) – which portrays the unfolding of a sub-continental tragedy in Radcliffe's dysentery-ridden haste of five weeks, his less-than-shoddy trifle of a scrawl that tore an entire country apart, uprooting millions from their hearth and home and leaving millions dead – can actually be *seen* operating in this neighbourhood, transcending both time and context.

> *The locale is the echo*
> *of a final answer.*
> *Sometimes they ask where it is.*
> *And then it surfaces like suppressed guilt*
> *on the city's face...*

At forty now, I am startled to see how this neighbourhood survives its fragmentedness, how it still breathes in us, real and imagined. I wonder whether it is this that gives it the tenacity to go on despite the slow, largely undocumented exodus of its inhabitants into that evermore unhomely elsewhere; the current skyline of chicken-coop structures that have come up as a result of the phenomena of rent and the increase in demands for flats; the road that gets widened in the hungry craze for cars, making walking a hazard, disconnecting people almost entirely from its pleasures.

I turn away from my window and write, slowly, in my notebook:

It's that pure devastation of picking the gilded frame that defines absence, speaks the name of tomorrow's dead sea. Extinction. Warm-blooded fur turning sepia in albums and talks. On certain afternoons, watching a leaden sky hanging low against the bars of this prison, we go eye-rolling-smug complaining of May's rain-cold; now, we cannot even bear imagining the hill's winters. We dole out concern to the man; suggest the woman glean joy from the season's flowers until we arrive again.

We perform well, for, each year the sadness grows less in the act. We've almost healed from wondering why utensils look unfamiliar always; cabinets feel strange to the touch; why the wooden floor, dead ancestor, slips back into childhood, tripping us over until we've learned to walk again, out of the body, into water.

We check in, annual guests, beaming stupid with vacation plans. Come evening, father's shadow will crawl to the ends of the earth for the firmest fish, the tenderest mutton, the best rice. At night he'll be sick with so much running. At dawn, mother will emerge drawing out old recipes from her heart; we have arrived with the world's hunger at our famished moorings. And inside the ventricle, time's frenzied hooves racing away to darkness; our eyes in our tongues, our tongues in our feet, scouring, sniffing, scavenging for a whiff of womb. But it's alright. This time, we'll place an order for pumpkin-seed curry and dry-fish chutney to keep ourselves buoyed.

A smile suffers on the wind's pursed lips, the sky in a neighbour's greeting. The light of questions tuned to music breaking into scar. Where are you these days? When did you arrive? For how long will you be here? The house shines with lost savings and the roof is a hilly-roof red, as we'd so wanted it to be. Nothing but the hilly-roof red, we had told the man from thousands of years away; we, the inheritors of his rain. And please don't let out the living room and turn the house into a tunnel we have to enter by the backyard like thieves. We've entered the garden where another April has vanished into weeds. But where is a house in a place that never was; where a garden, with bodies on the edge of dream?

SAMANTHA WYNNE-RHYDDERCH

Tree Tai Chi

Tree Tai Chi I: Larch

Who could tell whether it's ascending, that larch
or descending the cliff? Either way it's a shimmying larch.

We're used to seeing it shake blackbirds out of its hair
on windy days in March. I call it 'the larking larch'.

When the music of the rain stops, it finds itself
at the edge of the field miming a lurching larch.

It spells the letter Y with its two remaining arms
without knowing why, has no understanding it'll arch.

This is tree tai chi *flex the sky*. But how far can you flex
before you fall over, Wyn, are no longer a larch?

Tree Tai Chi 2: Oak

If you are a tree, how does time pass
when everything happens at such a slow pace?

That an oak can be stripped of all greenery by June
may be unusual but well known in this place.

Even if you're an oak that's 200 years old,
you won't be able to hold on at this unholy pace.

Once clay starts to crack in drought or slide in rain,
it releases every root. Here that's commonplace.

How much land are we losing? It's disappearing
at the rate of a metre a year. Which is a fair old pace.

What does it mean to live without ever leaving
the place you were born? Ask an oak about pace.

Arms raised in the shape of the letter V carved
with an L and two vowels in its bowed carapace.

Not a joke. This was once an oak. Now it's waving
goodbye to the list of who loved who in this space.

So busy doing tree tai chi *gazing at the moon*
they didn't notice the tide racing towards the coppice.

You may have the heart of an oak but that won't
save you from drowning, man. At your own pace.

Tree Tai Chi 3: Beech

We're all agreed trees need access to water
but what beech wants to be berthed in water?

Changed weather patterns can cause clay to give way.
Our boundary of beeches seem to be asleep in water.

This beech tree is demonstrating tree tai chi *between
heaven and earth* contorted in three feet of water.

Fish can't see dolphins in this miso soup of branches and mud.
Dolphins echolocate them. Then creep up on them underwater.

Murky water attracts pods of dolphins who teach their young
to find fish when they're concealed by clay in the water.

This tree seems half-beech half-dolphin as it prepares to backflip
off the cliff edge. One leg spelling J for Joy, it leaps into the water.

Tree Tai Chi 4: Apple Tree

There they go, staggering around, our apple trees,
like an orchard drunk on the fruit from its own trees.

One is arthritic, magnetised by the sea's sweet nothings;
another believes erosion does not apply to apple trees.

The one in the corner is flirting with the edge, whispering
to the dribble of shale on the beach below its family trees.

Are these petrified in the tai chi pose *row the boat*?
They must've moved yet we never see them shift, the trees.

One tree is doing a handstand spelling the first letter of anxiety.
This one's just a scribble against the sky. That's poetry.

Death watch

Who is that tapping? Who's trying to get through
to us five brothers keeping watch all night through?

The call of insect morse is insistent drilling which
our dying dad has known his whole life through.

The sheets that bandage his thin limbs and white
beaked head to the bed are soaked right through.

He looks like Old Father Time who has stopped ticking
in the four poster beetles have chewed through.

Like aristocrats, death watch beetles prefer the aged oak
of landed estates and warm nights in June to mate through.

These rafters, already 400 years dead were home
to forest birds for 200 years straight through.

The beetles' teeth chisel their way closer. Dad's dentures
rattle in a glass when one of us tries to tiptoe through.

This panelled room contains him like a coffin
the beetles have started eating through.

As his ninety years diminish to minutes it's hard to take in
this man will be a habitat for others to bite through.

Given they outnumber us Rodericks fifty to one,
best to live alongside them the next decade through.

Time

On occasions it feels compressed, does time,
at others dragging its feet one at a time.

It's a squeezebox bookended by two hands –
neither of them mine. Not that I was aware at the time.

For a minute the player holds the moment open
so the box can release each syllable at the allotted time.

Like the voices of ghosts stuck in its throat, the concertina
contains a choir which will sing if we all beat time.

Time seems a staircase we sled down as children
on a mattress, or bounded up like deer two at a time.

No gaps around the table then. How can we guess
we will descend on a stretcher in someone else's time?

Even if you forget to wind the clock or break its hands
it will still keep passing behind your back. In no time.

Or else it's a Slinky which holds its spirals close
till one touch gives it permission to defy time.

One day it lands at your feet in a neat coil.
Someone else will have to set it going: you're out of time.

You can't cajole or distract it: hours have their own
momentum. Which gets me every time.

If you dampen the sand in the egg timer it'll solidify
into that little cove I haven't seen in the longest time.

Fast forward to a night in November when our house
slipped off the cliff and we got out just in time.

As if the house had tripped? Well, we knew it would
because coastal erosion is just a matter of time.

For years the sundial in the garden pointed to the sea.
Then it started accusing the sky. Like it was outside time.

Weird how the montbretia still rush out every spring
at the spot where our back door was, even after all this time.

So there you have it. Good to see you and thank you
for the pint, Sam. Got to go. They've just called time.

STEWART SANDERSON

The Cheviots: A Future History

2121

Forty or fifty years after my ashes
have been scattered on its summit, Cheviot
will still be here, as so much else will not –
a hill across whose dark flank refugees
slip north by night, fleeing dystopias
and praying the last democratic state
left this side of Kaliningrad will let
them live in safety with their families.

Behind barbed wire, one country's border force
will scan another's through their sniper scopes
and send up drones to probe the other side
as every now and then small wars flare up
to smoulder for a week amidst the gorse
with casualties officially denied.

2221

Another century: how warm is it?
Did we perhaps avert catastrophe?
Or has the heather all been blazed away
from my beloved hills, gorse set alight
after successive summers gone without
enough rain falling, till one parched July
a *fyreflaucht* (hold the word close) left the sky
to choke the College Burn below with soot?

The optimist in me imagines flowers –
a glamour of strange petals in the waste
places, seeds borne from southern latitudes
in birds' stomachs. Perhaps once all the fires
die down, new colours will replace what's lost
and somehow Cheviot will be renewed.

2321

Under a cadmium-coloured sky, the hills
are bare now and these days few humans dare
climb too high up their blasted slopes for fear
of radiation bursts, the air which kills
scorching their lungs. A cumulus stack sails
high over Schil, not grey-white anymore
but pulsing with a dark, chemical fire
fit to be written into Dante's hells.

Down in the valleys, people hide behind
enviro-seals and concrete three feet thick
hoping the acid sleet and poisoned wind
won't eat into the wall by night and break
through with a sharp, fissiperating sound
heard for a second, should they chance to wake.

2421

A bleached bone, perfect on the high approach
to Blackhaggs Rigg, with nothing else to say
how it happened to be there as the day
diminishes over the Eastern March –
the first star shining faintly, like a brooch
emerging from the heavens' scoured soil high
above this pale form, partly buried by
fluorescent sands, which constantly encroach.

Impossible to know, at this distance
if it belonged to some species whose grip
on life has slipped, unable to resolve
the contradictions of its own existence
or one which, casting off a former shape,
is only now beginning to evolve.

2521

Whatever else occurs, I hope we are
part of this place's future; that it stays
a part of ours no matter what strange ways
we wander, straying perilously near
to our own end perhaps, but winning clear
with just enough time left for histories
to carry on; for unborn poets to praise
this land I love simply for being here.

Five hundred years from now, I hope we've learned
to be a better version of ourselves
and that not everything we are has burned.
With or without us, this landscape at least
will last – and as our warming world revolves
that thought tempts me towards a kind of peace.

PHIL COPE

Beyond Coal

An extract from *The Golden Valley: a visual biography of the Garw Valley* (Seren, 2021)

Any biography of the Garw must start, not with coalmining which has become the whole of the tale though little more than a hundred year blip, less than a chronological flicker ... but with its hills and with its water. The land's best conjuring trick is its river always emptying itself but always full, snaking from countless springs, before and still along the belly of the valley, taking the steeply sloping land's easiest path, never uncertain in its simple objective, serpent-like in our once- and possibly-future Garden of Eden.

The valleys of the south Wales coalfield, separated by high passes, with poor transport networks (and, in the case of the 'dead-end' Garw, no passing traffic at all), set alongside the lack of large areas of flat ground upon which to build has minimised the kinds of employment initiatives, post coal, which see the footprints of giant factories as the only solution.

We need to be imagining a very different kind of future, laid out in human trails and bicycle tracks; in accommodation and decent places for visitors to eat and to drink; in Kevin Sinnott's art, and Workmen's Hall performances; and in the re-opening of the railway; with all of our energy supplied from mountain-top turbines, blown by our nearly-always-available wind.

As history has made an about-turn in my cul-de-sac home, we're already returning, after coal, to a more traditional relationship with the land. In a combination of humankind's efforts to say sorry and nature's own unstoppable reclamation scheme, greater celandine and common valerian, creeping buttercup and wood sorrel are flowering like parables through the cracks in Garw's ruins, suggesting something possible; and bramble, broom and common gorse, feverfew and primrose are rising up in nature's quiet fight-back.

Our new lakes are alive again with brown trout and frogs, with dragonflies, ducks and dippers, coots and moorhens, and the always solitary and antisocial heron. And a peregrine falcon couple make their annual visit here, in a good year, nesting confident in a wall of quarried cliffs where stone was once cut to build miners' houses.

The land has remained – beaten up, of course, its flesh in places gored – but wounds heal, with the days of coal mining now as unimaginable to most of us as the ages of ice, or those of the building of the ancient cairns on the surrounding hills to bury the dead. And even if, after all of our efforts, none of our most recent and dreamed-of schemes for survival work out for our complex and contradictory species ... no matter. The grass, the trees, the bushes will soon grow high through the windows of our abandoned homes and shops, rising through the floorboards of our churches, schools, and workmen's halls, flourishing once again where they always used to flourish.

And the extremophile lichen on the rocks of the burial chambers of our Bronze Age ancestors will continue to spread like glorious, radiating stains. These, in truth, were always the real survivors anyway, tolerant of desert heat and arctic cold, of irradiation, pollution, and even being shot into space ... so coalmining's brief century of much gentler poisonings has left little more than a mark on them.

In a 1987 interview – just two years after the closure of the last pit in the Garw – Margaret Thatcher proclaimed that, there was 'no such thing as society', just individuals and their families, ushering in a decade and more of the politics of individualism. A similar debate is now raging concerning the nature of lichens and of the myriad other formations of the fungi family. When you look closely at these ancient organisms, it's difficult to tell if they are single creatures or a vast collective; individuals or one being, grouped closely together for safety.

Ninety per cent of the world's plants depend on mycorrhizal connections (*mykes*, Greek for fungus / *rhiza*, root), linking them in vast underground networks with nearly every organism, passing carbon, water, nutrients like phosphorus and nitrogen, and even alarm signals back and forth through their elaborate circuitries, in what Richard Powers has termed an 'underground welfare state' [from *The Overstory*, 2018].

English botanist David Read named these fine, tubular structures that branch, fuse and tangle in an almost-infinite filigree below our feet, the 'Wood-Wide Web', challenging Darwinian hegemony of the 'survival of the fittest' as the best description for the workings of the natural world, as well as Adam Smith's championing of selfish individualism in a free market.

These old/new lessons are crystal clear within the smallest and the largest of things. Intensive commercial forestry practices which select and plant only what is thought to be the most profitable of trees – expelling in the process most species of bird, mammal and insect life, and ripping up much of the land's underground communication and support system – have resulted in much less lucrative yields with much more vulnerability to disease ... as well as featureless, dark and silent arboreal deserts. Perhaps, from lichens and trees to cities and human relationships, theirs is a more useful way to understand and thrive within our world.

Mutual aid and co-operation were essential for people's survival in the Garw, when intolerable forces were applied to lives and to the land during the harsh years of coalmining. The construction, equipping and running of workmen's halls and institutes, and the establishment of mutual aid societies were based upon the principle that the health of the individual was most effectively guaranteed by the well-being of the whole ... with no one left behind. In this co-operation-for-survival model – paralleled by what we are learning about the reciprocity and even altruism of the superorganism of forest and field – the healthy paid for the sick, the working for the unemployed.

And it is this spirit that is being recalled, in some small ways today, in our communitarian responses to the new realities of the Covid-19 pandemic, which only a united co-evolutionary response will defeat, a reaction which begins, perhaps, to track a path towards a new future for the people of the Garw, as well as everywhere else.

The coal, which brought droves of men and their families to this tiny valley a little over a century ago, took 250 million years to create. While decaying trees and plants were swamped and compressed – every twenty feet of vegetable debris producing just one foot of coal – it took us less than a hundred years to exhaust it.

But despite this and other alarming evidence, and in the knowledge that we have now entered the Holocene Age, the sixth mass extinction period of our planet, the lichen and the rocks of the Garw Valley, its river, trees and hills, its birds and fish, its animals, insects and fungi will win ... always were winning, really, despite appearances. After taking their beating, it's clear that the earth is blooming again, one blade at a time through our detritus of brick and coal and greed.

And, as the sun continues to rise and fall over our golden valley, the only real question for us today is whether we will decide to throw our weight behind the inevitably-victorious team ... or not.

ROBERT MINHINNICK

Parc Calon Lan Suite, Blaengarw

after Daniel James (Gwyrosydd) & John Hughes
for Phil Cope

Mynydd Llangeinwyr

Elevation   568 m (1,864 ft)
Prominence   90 m (300 ft)
Listing   sub-HuMP, County top

Coordinates
51.6412°N 3.5726°W
            Coordinates: 51.6412°N
                          3.5726°W

Location   Bridgend, Wales
OS grid   SS 912947

1.

Coal?
The roof fell in.
If we listen carefully
we may still hear
grief in its strict metres.

2.

Language?
Tight as a shackle
tying the deacons to their doxology.
But only sheep's wool on barbed wire now –
vanished like their tabernacle.

3.

4.

Rubbing our eyes
not robbing our eyes

at a dragonfly above the Garw source
– spring or seepage still unsure –

because it takes hundreds of springs to make one river
but the people who create the cists and the cairns

and the axe factory amongst the thistles
and shrooms must choose locations carefully

rubbing their eyes
and rubbing their eyes

between Steep Holm and Pen y Fan
and Gwyr and the Gwrhyd

as for one day only
or maybe two in their year

the air clears
and they find the world is stretching...

until it is stranger than
Cornwall, Phoenicia, Amerika...

and melting because ... Ah!
The psychedelics of sight...

5.

I'm not asking for a life of luxury
because Heol Alecsandra *yn llawn daioni*
and Studio 18 *yn llawn daioni*
and Blaengarw Workmen's Hall *yn llawn daioni*
and Y Tabernacl *yn llawn daioni*
and The Royal Hotel *yn llawn daioni*
and Ocean Colliery memorial marker *yn llawn daioni*
and Fforchwen farm *yn llawn daioni*
and Forest View 209 metres above sea level *yn llawn daioni*
and the Assirati's from Bardi *yn llawn daioni*
and Corilla Plastics *yn llawn daioni*
and Parc Calon lan yn llawn daioni
for only a pure heart is able to sing this way
singing at night and singing through the day...

6.

Corn Du to Picws Du
and millennia later
the unnameables possess names
miraculously out of language chemistry
but those places had already become ideas
in the old geezers' minds
and beyond the beyond
a beach like the chief old geezer's yellow coat
and later twelve farms are built
until the steam coal reveals itself
and then the forests are sown over the farms,
black sitka on their needlebeds
beloved of arsonists and speedway boys
– dragonflies themselves –
and now in masks we drive along
Gwendoline Street and Katie Street
and Oxford Street and Tymeinwr Avenue
and the streetparties are full swing
and another clear morning arrives
on our scratchcard planet
and we stand rubbing our eyes not robbing our eyes
at the people knocking off from the parachute factory
and a second shift signing on to pack the gorgeous silks
walking away and walking home
and there is thistledown in the darkness,
its wraiths around us
in King Edward Street and Pwllcarn Terrace
and I know these invisibles are everywhere...
but they are still following a leader's yellow coat...

BIOGRAPHIES

Abeer Ameer's poems have appeared in print and online journals and anthologies. She is a recipient of the Literature Wales Mentoring Scheme for 2020. Her debut collection *Inhale/Exile* in which she shares stories of her Iraqi forebears is available from Seren Books. She lives in Cardiff.

Aditi Angiras is a writer and artist based in New Delhi. She is co-editor of *The World That Belongs to Us: An Anthology of Queer Poetry from South Asia* (HarperCollins India, 2020).

Priya Sarukkai Chabria is based in Pune, India. Her books include the just released *Sing of Life: Revisioning Tagore's Gitanjali* (poems), *Andal: The Autobiography of a Goddess* (translation), *Clone* (speculative fiction) and *Bombay/Mumbai: Immersions* (non-fiction). She has received the Muse Translation Award and been recognised for her Outstanding Contribution to Literature by the Government of India.

Sampurna Chattarji is a poet, fiction-writer, translator, and editor. Her twenty books include the short story collection about Bombay/Mumbai, *Dirty Love* (Penguin); the novels *Rupture* and *Land of the Well* (both from HarperCollins); translations of Joy Goswami's poetry – *After Death Comes Water* and *Selected Poems* (both in Harper Perennial); and nine poetry titles. Her latest poetry collection is *Space Gulliver: Chronicles of an Alien* (HarperCollins 2020). She lives in Thane, Maharashtra.

Phil Cope writes about the sacred springs and holy wells of Wales, England, Scotland, Cornwall and Ireland. As well as these, Phil has books published on themes as diverse as Haitian vodou, Paul Robeson, the Spanish Civil War and the Olympic and Paralympic Games. His most recent volume is *The Golden Valley* (Seren, 2021), about Cwm Garw, where he created the Valley and Vale Community Arts initiative and he still lives.

Tishani Doshi publishes poetry, essays and fiction. Her most recent books are *Girls Are Coming Out of the Woods,* shortlisted for the Ted Hughes Award, and a novel, *Small Days and Nights,* shortlisted for the RSL Ondaatje Prize. For fifteen years she worked as a dancer with the Chandralekha group in Chennai. Her fourth collection of poetry is *A God At the Door* (Bloodaxe, 2021) is Forward Prize-nominated. She lives in a coastal village in Tamil Nadu, where the name of her beachside house, *Ar Lan y Môr* ('Beside the Sea'), provides a physical expression of her Welsh-Gujarati heritage.

Peter Finch is a poet, author and critic who lives in Cardiff. He is author of the Real Cardiff books, and editor of the 'Real' series, published by Seren. *The Machineries of Joy* is his latest poetry collection.

Mandy Haggith lives in Assynt, Scotland, and teaches Literature and Creative Writing at the University of the Highlands and Islands. Her eleven books include an Iron Age historical novel trilogy, The Stone Stories, and four poetry collections.

Suzanne Iuppa is a poet, community worker and film-maker who lives in Aberangell, north Wales. She grew up on Lake Ontario and now co-ordinates Renew Wales activities in north Powys as a way to reduce the impact of climate change in her region.

Mike Jenkins is a poet and short-story writer who lives in Merthyr Tudful. A former editor of *Poetry Wales*, he has won the Wales Book of the Year (1998). Jenkins is editor of the annual Red Poets. Some of his work is in Merthyr dialect.

Nabanita Kanungo is a writer and geographer based in Shillong, India. She has written essays and articles on aspects of urban culture, landscape and memory, developmental economics and geo-ecological history. Kanungo is also the author of two collections of poetry – *A Map of Ruins* (Sahitya Akademi, 2014) and *159* (Poetrywala, 2018).

Christopher Meredith's most recent publications are *Still* (poetry) and *Please* (novel) both from Seren in 2021. A critical book about his writing was published by University of Wales Press in 2018. His first novel, *Shifts*, is a Seren Classic. He lives in Brecon.

Robert Minhinnick is co-founder of Friends of the Earth Cymru and Sustainable Wales/Cymru Gynaliadwy. He published *Green Agenda: Essays on the Environment of Wales* (Seren) in 1994. He lives in Porthcawl. Minhinnick is pleased to acknowledge the influence of Peter Finch on 'Parc Calon Lan Suite, Blaengarw'.

Samantha Wynne-Rhydderch is a poet from west Wales with collections from Seren and Picador and pamphlets from Redbeck and Rack Press. She lives in Cei Newydd, Ceredigion, where she teaches creative writing.

Stewart Sanderson is a poet from Scotland. Author of two pamphlets – *Fios* (2015) and *An Offering* (2018) – his first full collection, *The Sleep Road*, will be published by Tapsalteerie in October 2021.

Laura Wainwright's first poetry pamphlet is *Air and Armour* (Green Bottle Press, 2021). She has a PhD from Cardiff University and is the author of the literary-critical book, *New Territories in Modernism: Anglophone Welsh Writing, 1930-49* (University of Wales Press, 2018). Wainwright lives in Newport, south Wales.

ACKNOWLEDGEMENTS

Our thanks to the editors of *New Welsh Review* and *Blackbox Manifold* which first published 'Ffynnon Wen', 'The Holy Power of Penylan' and 'Suite at Parc Calon Lan'; to Seren Books for permission to include 'Steampunk Jungle' from Christopher Meredith's *Still* (2021) and an extract from Phil Cope's *The Golden Valley* (2021);

To Happenstance Press and Tapsalteerie Press for their advice.

Also, to David Thomas and Bill Hopkins, a loving couple from south Wales, whose generosity has enabled a second volume of *Gorwelion Shared Horizons* to be considered.

To Christine Eynon and Merryn Hutchings, for their continued generosity to Sustainable Wales / Cymru Gynaliadwy; and to Parthian Books itself.

PARTHIAN *Poetry/Prose*

'A lovely book...
Read and enjoy,
I certainly did.'
IOLO WILLIAMS

Riverwise: Meditations on Afon Teifi
JACK SMYLIE WILD
ISBN 978-1913640-39-2
£9 | Paperback

'(A) fine, absorbing and wonderfully attentive book' – **Nation.Cymru**

'Reading *Riverwise*, we are reminded to find meaning in what truly matters' – **Wales Arts Review**

'*Riverwise* is profoundly personal ... based on real knowledge and love, and is mercifully free from moralising.' – ***The Lady***

Riverwise is a book of wanderings and wonderings, witnessings and enchantments, rememberings and endings. Weaving memoir, poetry and keen observation into its meandering course, it shifts across time and space to reflect the beauty of hidden, fluvial places, and to meditate on the strangeness of being human.

A clarion call to learn to love and protect the natural world and its waterways.

PARTHIAN *Poetry*

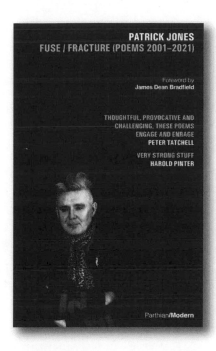

fuse / fracture
(poems 2001-2021)
PATRICK JONES
ISBN 978-1-913640-42-2
£10 | Paperback

'Very strong stuff' – **Harold Pinter**

'Thoughtful, provocative and
challenging, these poems engage and
enrage.'
– **Peter Tatchell**

Windfalls
SUSIE WILD
ISBN 978-1-912681-75-4
£9 | Paperback

'Powerful, beautifully crafted poems'
– Jonathan Edwards

'a magpie's appetite for glimpsed moments.'
– *Western Mail*

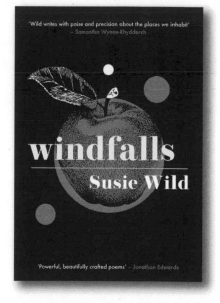